Richard Chandler

Rhymes for the Ranks

soldiers' songs & sonnets

Richard Chandler

Rhymes for the Ranks
soldiers' songs & sonnets

ISBN/EAN: 9783337271756

Printed in Europe, USA, Canada, Australia, Japan

Cover: Foto ©Andreas Hilbeck / pixelio.de

More available books at **www.hansebooks.com**

RHYMES FOR THE RANKS

(SOLDIERS' SONGS & SONNETS).

BY

RICHARD CHANDLER.

" (Their's) the blunt speech that bursts without a pause,
And freeborn thoughts which league the Soldier with the Laws."

Scott—Vision of Don Roderick.

London:

T. BOSWORTH, 198, HIGH HOLBORN.

1875.

C. ROWLAND BROWN, PRINTER, 40, SUN STREET, FINSBURY, E.C.

TO

H.R.H. THE DUKE OF CAMBRIDGE,

COMMANDER-IN-CHIEF OF THE BRITISH ARMY,

THIS UNWORTHY TESTIMONIAL TO THE PROWESS OF THAT ARMY IS

(By permission)

RESPECTFULLY DEDICATED.

CONTENTS.

———————

In Memoriam.

YE soldiers of our fatherland,
　　Who prompt my simple lays,
The exploits ye have wrought require
　　No humble minstrel's praise.

The memory of your deeds shall last
　　As long as lasts the sun;
That orb which ceaseless wakes to life,
　　The noontide British gun.

Staunch soldiers of our fatherland,
　　Oft hath the tale been told,
Of calm, resolved, determined deeds
　　Ye did in days of old.

The sun that gleams on tower and dome,
　No humble cot disdains;
Though Lords of Song your valour hymn,
　Accept my humble strains.

The subjects of immortal verse,
　I seek with rhyme to wed;
How much has been but faintly told—
　How much left still unsaid.

Oft have I turned my murky glass,
　To catch the rays that shine
Round Britain's flag, but dropped the hand—
　No worthy mirror mine.

Brave soldiers of our fatherland,
　Who prompt my simple lays;
Accept the tribute, poor and weak,
　A humble minstrel prays.

THE PIONEER.

WHERE burns the midnight taper,
    And numbers halt or flow;
The coffers of my wealth consist
    Of many a volumed row;
Above, the Iron Duke regards
    The fruits of peace below.

Of all the simple ornaments,
    My homely walls that grace,
The likeness of the Iron Duke
    Enjoys the highest place—
And not alone for artist's sake
    I love that war-worn face.

Where fickle sunbeams darting
    O'er many a chimney tall,
Review a Falstaff's regiment
    Of bundles great and small;
The portrait of the Iron Duke,
    Alone adorns my wall.

'Tis but a fond Utopia,
　　The dream of constant peace,
Wherever wealth increases,
　　The foes of wealth increase;
The very rest the soldier earns,
　　Is guarded by police.

So love I well the warrior,
　　The terror of the foe,
He ranks among my household gods,
　　My civic gods also—
That war-worn face regarding
　　The fruits of peace below.

A PARABLE FOR ALL TIME.

'TWAS at an ancient hostel,
  In a quaint old fashioned street,
One placid summer's evening
  Two strangers chanced to meet.

The one he was a trader,
  A ring of gold he wore;
Of angels and of costly wares
  He had a goodly store.

The other was a soldier,
  In homely garb arrayed,
Of giant limb, and fitting port
  To lead a cavalcade.

These strangers made a bargain,
  Who sang the ruder lay
In honour of his mistress,
  The other's score should pay.

Within that ancient hostel,
  A tuned Theorbo hung;
And to a pleasant measure,
  'Twas thus the trader sung :—

" I love, I love a maiden,
With pearls her locks are laden,
    The emerald and sapphire deck her dainty,
        dainty throat;
And gems the best and rarest
Adorn her hand—the fairest;
    The jewels on her stomacher my lady's wealth
        denote.

" Her voice is soft and winning,
(Can gold be ever sinning)
    And only pearls can rival her ruby-resting teeth;
Her eyes when brightly beaming
Like diamonds are streaming,
    A flood of light on lesser sparks that glitter
        thick beneath.

" Oh! richly dowered maiden,
With every virtue laden,
    I would! I would! thy beauty choice and
        costly gear were mine;
Thy locks so bright and sunny
(Of kindred hue to money),
    With Ophir's richest products I freely would
        entwine."

So ceased with measured cadence,
    The comely cheping man.
At once with careless accents,
    The soldier thus began :—

"I love, I love a beldam,
Her smile she sheweth seldom,
   She pranketh not in rich brocade or any dainty
      gear;
Of visage she is toothless;
Of temper she is ruthless;
   And whosoe'er regards her is apt to shrink
      with fear.

"She breatheth not of spices;
Her's are no courtier's vices;
   Her lay of love is terrible, her hue is aught
      but fair;
'Tis only steel that dights her,
And war alone delights her;
   No jewels deck her iron form, no pearls adorn
      her hair.

"Yet lacks she not a wooer,
Though gallants none pursue her,
   And well she guards another's wares she careth
      not to taste;
Thy jewelled maid and golden
To her is much beholden,
   Right well the soldier loves to clutch her meagre
      wiry waist."

Then ope'd the comely trader
   The gypscire that he bore,
And with a smile acquitted,
   The soldier's modest score.

THE ENGLISHMAN'S DOMAIN.

(Was ist des Deutschen Vaterland?)

WHAT is the Englishman's domain?
    The narrow land four seas contain?
Or Caledonia's mountains wild?
Or Erin, ocean's wayward child?
In vain! in vain! in vain!
To limit thus his vast domain.

Is it where Polar currents freeze?
Or Hallowed Isle of northern seas?
Where table mountain scares the plain?
Or Calpe frowns on fretful Spain?
In vain! in vain! in vain!
To limit thus his vast domain.

Is't where Bermuda's corals smile?
Or Aden's sand, or Malta's isle?
Is't home of Sikh, or proud Afghan?
Or subtle sensuous Hindostan?
In vain! in vain! in vain!
To limit thus his vast domain.

What is the Englishman's domain?
Is't Himalaya's mountain chain?
Or Western Afric's storm-tossed beach?
Or where New Zealand's forests reach?
In vain! in vain! in vain!
To limit thus his vast domain.

What is the Englishman's domain?
Acadia, haunt of peaceful swain,
Australia's young, but grand extent,
An island and a continent;
In vain! in vain! in vain!
To limit thus his vast domain.

What is the Englishman's domain?
Where peace brings justice in her train;
Where honour springs, and truth is bred;
Where treason dare not show her head;
Where glory calls, nor calls in vain,
There is the Briton's proud domain.

A RANDOM TEAR.

FIE, boy fie! a tear in the eye?
   Heroes are made of sterner stuff;
Lassie so dear! truce to the tear,
   Why has a soldier's sleeve a cuff?

Fie, boy fie! twelve years gone by,
   Medals so gay on your breast will shine;
Right about face, a breathing space,
   "Lads of the awkward squad form line!"

Right! boy right! your face is bright,
   Hope is the soldier's guiding star;
Where colours fly and glory's nigh,
   There is your home wherever you are.

PIPECLAY AND SALT.

YOU may talk of your Graces and Muses,
  The wooing of moonlight and wave,
Here's a toast—curse the clown who refuses,
  The love of the brave for the brave;
So drink it in whiskey, Jamaica, or malt
The union perpetual of pipeclay and salt.

The ivy the oak may embrace, sir,
  The woodbine the hawthorn may tie,
But for beauty and delicate grace, sir,
  With the services neither can vie;
So drink it in whiskey, Jamaica, or malt,
The union perpetual of pipeclay and salt.

As a grenadier, who is so smart, sir?
  A sailor, so lissome and free?
A soldier's as straight as a dart sir?
  And Jack, who's so supple as he?
The sun never sees from the Zodiac's vault
Two substances match like true pipeclay and salt.

On the land 'tis our firmness we trust in,
  On the sea 'tis their dash that we prize,
When the salt is our bayonets crustin'
  Then hurrah for our naval allies!
So drink it in whiskey, Jamaica, or malt,
The union perpetual of pipeclay and salt.

There are nosegays of water and land, sir,
  And flowers of most delicate hue,
No tricolour fairer you scanned, sir,
  Than red, sailors' ducks, and true blue;
So drink it in whiskey, Jamaica, or malt,
The union perpetual of pipeclay and salt.

Old Jove is the god of the earth, sir,
  And Neptune's the god of the sea,
Olympus ne'er witnessed such mirth, sir,
  As when Mars joined the two in a glee;
So drink it in whiskey, Jamaica, or malt,
The union perpetual of pipeclay and salt.

Where there's land for our colours to fly on,
  Or seas for our navies to sweep,
Here's a cheer for the heroes we dote on,
  The lords of the dry and the deep;
So drink it in whiskey, Jamaica, or malt,
The union perpetual of pipeclay and salt.

LE PETIT TAMBOUR.

ONLY just a drummer boy!
  Stranger, who are you?
Pray regard this little toy—
  Nothing to the view.
Stick on parchment makes a noise—
Follow all the bearded boys.

Aide-de-camp and adjutant
  Holloa till they're hoarse;
Brigadier and commandant
  Are but men of course.
"Tap, tap, tap!" I beat my drum—
No mistake! each man must come.

Flags! they've got no sort of sound,
  Don't think much about 'em,
Sergeants compass them around,
  Troops *can* do without 'em.
Nobles of the bluest blood
Listen for the drummer's thud.

True, I am but four feet six.
  Hearken, I implore ye,
Marshals, when I twirl my sticks,
  Learn the road to glory.
Though with darkness all be dumb,
Ceaseless rolls the British drum.

OUR COLONEL.

A Turk, some thought our Colonel,
　　Parade and drill eternal;
But praise from him was worth a limb,
　　That martinet, our Colonel.

A muff, some thought our Colonel,
　　Absorbed in book or journal—
Of martial lore how great lies store
　　Our simple, silent Colonel.

A brick, all knew our Colonel,
　　When volleyed fires infernal—
On rank and file, how sweet his smile,
　　Our calm, collected Colonel.

Ubique quo Fas et Gloria ducunt.

FILL high your cups, my merry men,
    Be this your toast to-night:
The lads in blue, of courage true,
    Found everywhere for right.
Everywhere for right, my boys,
    Everywhere for right;
North, south, east, west, have oft' confessed
    The British gunner's might.

The signal-sound of strife, my boys,
    Our iron-voices roar;
Nor foot, nor horse, a passage force,
    But round shot goes before.
Here, there, everywhere,
    In watch and ward, and fight;
The cannon's mouth, east, west, north, south,
    Is witness for the right.

There's glory in the battle's din,
    There's glory in pursuit;
On Fame's Gazette, the type is set,
    Whene'er our guns salute.
Everywhere for right, my boys,
    Everywhere for right;
Old world and new, the red and blue
    Have often had in sight.

THE BLUES.

TOIL, march, and countermarch,
    Picket, guard, and sentry,
How I curse the moment, when
    The service saw my entry;
Worked and worn, become the prey
    Of many a sad misgiving,
Many knocks for little pay,
    Life's not worth the living.

Toil, march, and countermarch,
    Night and day no leisure,
Slave to articles of war
    Dying were a pleasure;
Curses on the uniform,
    Source of my misgiving—
Hark! the pickets are engaged,
    No such fun as living.

THAT UGLY MAN FROM NOTTINGHAM.

THAT ugly man from Nottingham
　　Who made the Regiment laugh,
So pungent in his pleasantries,
　　So happy in his chaff;
The evils of a soldier's life
　　However big they'd be,
He'd rout them by his raillery,
　　Or turn them by his glee.
No Doctor with dissecting knife,
　　Or Marshal with his staff,
Could match that man from Nottingham,
　　That made the Regiment laugh.
　　　　That ugly man from Nottingham, &c.

He'd rate a mouldy biscuit
　　'Till a Weevil hid his face,
The oldest grumbler guffawed at
　　His comical grimace;
Desertion from the service—
　　He knocked it down to half,
That ugly man from Nottingham,
　　That made the Regiment laugh.
　　　　That ugly man from Nottingham, &c.

No matter where his billet was,
    The crossest held him dear;
A Quaker brushed his uniform,
    Good Templars stood him beer;
He'd ape each creature 'neath the sun,
    From monkey to giraffe,
That ugly man from Nottingham,
    That made the Regiment laugh.
        That ugly man from Nottingham, &c.

In presence of the enemy,
    The mildest soldier born,
Would rather face a cannon than
    His withering words of scorn;
He'd put a sense of honour in
    The veriest riff raff,
That ugly man from Nottingham,
    Who made the Regiment laugh.
        That ugly man from Nottingham, &c.

THE SOLDIER SAINT.

ST George of Cappadocia
   Shall be the Saint for me,
His cross adorns the banner
   Of mighty Kingdoms three.

I honour Blessed Patrick,
   Saint Andrew I revere,
But Cappadocia's Warrior,
   The Soldier holds most dear.

Ho! Erin, thou wast reeling
   Beneath the Danish sway,
When triumph came and freedom,
   Upon Saint George's day.

Oft Scotia! thy marauders,
   Hied home with grevious loss,
When pealed the English war-shout,
   When waved Saint George's cross.

See, on the British Standard,
   The blazons fair entwined,
The symbols of three countries
   In amity combined.

And be the might of Britain
   From rise to set of sun,
When trumpets peal, and colours fly,
   Increased as three to one.

The Gaul may praise Saint Denis,
   Saint Iago, he of Spain,
Saint George's sacred symbol
   Is chief on land and main.

When lowers the front of battle,
   Wherever be the place,
The Sainted Soldier's banner
   Shall never know disgrace.

LOVE SONG.

MY bonny English lassie,
   Her merits who may tell;
The happy grace, the radiant face,
   Where sunbeams seem to dwell.

The port that speaks of freedom,
   The charming English smile,
The tongue that trips, 'twixt ruby lips,
   In ignorance of guile.

The cheek to shame a stranger,
   The eyes that dart a spell;
Her step how smart, how pure her heart,
   Who loves a soldier well.

What fondly fabled Houri,
   Or subtle southern Belle,
Can vie in grace with her sweet face,
   Who loves a soldier well.

BALACLAVA.

*" C'est très magnifique mais ce n'est pas
la guerre."*

THE scribbler in safety may fairly enlarge
　　On the blunders we made in that terrible
charge;
But the burst of our steeds, and the stroke of
our steel,
Caused the column to waver, the squadron to reel.
We were but six hundred; how many the foe,
We knew not, we asked not, we cared not to
know;
'Midst the flashing of cannon, the musketry's roll,
We heard but our orders, we saw but our goal.
The fire-fringèd mountains we shook with our
tread,
Front and flank were our foemen, behind us
our dead.
In a whirlwind of carnage the guns we rode
through,
For slaughter too many, for conquest too few.

Then breathless, but fearless, a passage we tore
Through a death-dealing host where our dead
  lay before.
It might not be war, the mad freak that we
  wrought—
To learn the result, ask the Russ what he thought—
Count the labyrinthed legions that studded the
  track,
Where a Regiment swept forth and a Troop
  straggled back.

THE LOSS OF THE " BIRKENHEAD."

SWIFTLY on her voyage sped,
    Taut and trim, the Birkenhead,
Richly she with cargo stored,
British soldiers were on board;
Uniforms, green, blue and red
Flaunted on the Birkenhead.
Afric's mountains lay before,
Tramp of war oppressed the shore;
Foemen threatened England's fame,
Swift and stern her answer came.
Ere another day had fled
Land would greet the Birkenhead;
Tinkling rose the Ocean's spray,
Died the seaman's song away.
Sleep, stout soldiers, sleep to night,
Labour woos you with the light.
    *   *   *   *
    *   *   *   *
Hark! a wild and awful crashing,
See, a world of waters dashing,
Rings the wild alarum cry—
"The ship has struck, we die! we die!"

Regiments discipline may bind,
Reigns supreme one master mind ;
Strangers to one common sway
Units naught but self obey :
Self—whose all absorbing spell—
Makes of man a fiend of hell,
Let but terror blanch the cheek
Instinct tramples down the weak.
'Midst the Babel loud and shrill
Yielding to a hero's will,
Rose the soldier-spirit high—
Ready, aye, to die and die.
Ceased the strife of man with man,
Order's holy reign began,
(Triumph of the nobly brave,
Man the victor—self the slave.)
Soon his place each soldier found,
Failed no dressing, broke no sound ;
Calm, as ever on parade,
Seton ordered—all obeyed.
Soon one fragile boat is lowered,
Shrieking women cower on board,
Sole she labours through the sea
Doubtful ark of safety she.
Rooted to each quivering plank
Not one soldier broke the rank,
(Noblest feat of fortitude,
Man the victor—fear subdued.)

Theme too dire for verse or prose,
Sinking vessel's dying throes;
Evil counsel well designed,
'Scaped the generous captain's mind
(Other hope of safety past
Not a selfish thought the last),
" Swimming, seek yon boat to gain,"
Noble Seton cried " Remain,
Any soldier's lightest weight
Dooms to death her precious freight."
Passed an instant, all was o'er,
Rang the victor Ocean's roar;
Rolled the waters wild and rude,
Sank a phalanx unsubdued;
Passed to God the martyr band,
Found they all a better land;
Lost to Britain's Muster Roll,
Christ receive each hero's soul.

THE AUTUMN MANŒUVRES, 1872.

By Lance-Corporal O'Grady, Kerry Militia.

OH! the Downs of Wiltshire, they are so
   charmin',
  More be-token Pewsey, where it always rains;
Where our money taken, kapes the cats in bacon,
  Where on a single line they run their thrains.
Faith it was charmin' to see the armin',
   The bridlein' and the bucklin', and the swearin'
    too,
When the hivy Throopers and the slim young
   Supers,
  Started at night to kape the foe in view.

When Mr. R————n, warn't he a proud un?
  Bouldly in darkness led 'em round and round;
Centre and wings, sir, made fairy rings, sir,
  And Giant Circles on the hills were found.
At dead of night, sir, they did affright, sir,
   The folks of Winterbourne upon the plain;
Lightnin' and thunder, made the natives wonder
  If that 'ere Boneypart weren't come again.

With mighty pain, sir, the throops did gain, sir,
  The Codford Rapids, near six inches deep;
But the judge assarted, too soon they started,
    And so they shut their eyes, sir, and went
    to sleep.
Oh! the Downs of Wiltshire, they are so charmin',
  Swate ladies fingers ticklin' souldiers' feet;
And the flags so swately fluttherin' where they
    kapes the bread and butther in,
    And the Lancers and the Prancers, and the
    corps they call *d'élite*.

Oh! the pretty girls at Wiley, that made eyes at
    us so slyly,
  And the lazy louts, their swatehearts, just as
    jealous as might be,
And the wiry Enniskillens, all the lads well
    worth their shillin's,
    With them pilferin' Scotch Militia and Sir
    Garnet Wol-se-ley.
Wiltshire Yeomen proudly pacin', with their horses
    fit for racin',
    And all the guns a roarin' which made the
    yokels stare;
And we broths of boys from Kerry, all soldierlike
    and merry,
    At twenty paces shootin' them North Glosters
    in the rare.

Then to see the Prince Apparin', and all the folks
  a charin',
  And thunderin' great Ambassadors, their horses
  houldin' tight;
With hares such boys to go, sir, all cuttin' like
  the foe, sir,
  We koindly gave em quarter and billets for
  the night.
But the sight was braver still, sir, that we had
  at Bacon Hill, sir,
  When our Regiment and the rest, sir, had a
  mighty foine review;
And the Marquises and Duchesses, and the folks
  that came on crutches'es,
  All left their houses impty jist to see what
  we could do.

Shure now I'm home in Kerry, it's a proud man
  I am, very,
  To count up all the miles of folks that looked
  at us galore;
Them Wiltshire lads that autumn, what a heap
  of things we taught 'em,
  To use their own varnaycular "they never
  knowed avore."

THE OLD COLOURS.

BEAR the honoured Standards high,
    O'er their rags the Zephyrs sigh;
Flaunt the remnants to the breeze,
They have known worse winds than these:
Rent and split by shell and shot,
Blast of battle thick and hot
Blew in tempest dire and black,
Never blew those colours back.
Zephyrs, fan them with your breath,
Theirs has been the path of death;
Path of honour, path of glory,
Path renowned in song and story.
Symbols they of all that's dear,
Pure and high in life's career;
Often round each Badge of pride,
Heroes conquered, heroes died.
Bear the honoured Standards nigh,
Who for England would not die?
Emblem apt, red, white, and blue,
Blood, and hope, and honour true.

Rainbow tints the brighter gleaming,
When no summer sun is beaming;
Lay the honoured symbols by
Where the anthem pealeth high.
Sympathetic let them wave
In the vaulted Minster nave;
Sermons they in lofty station,
On the Church's supplication.
"Peace, good Lord, in mercy send us,
For thou only canst defend us"—
Praise and glory render both,
To the Lord of Sabaoth.

HORSE ARTILLERY.

AN EPISODE.

WHERE *Honour's fountains* bubble clear
   The French sweep on in wild career,
O'erwhelmed by sabre and by spear—
   Alas for Norman Ramsay!

Before, behind, on either side,
The dashing troopers fiercely ride,
And onward pour in martial pride—
   Alas for Norman Ramsay!

A lion caught in hunter's net,
A sapphire small in brilliants set,
Hemmed in, cut off, undaunted yet—
   Small hope for Norman Ramsay!

Then cracked the whip, then whirled the blade,
And drivers swore, and horses neighed,
As to and fro the foemen swayed—
   Hot work with Norman Ramsay!

Hurrah! the surging squadrons reel,
A sea of dust, a din of steel,
And through they burst with whizzing wheel—
   Hurrah for Norman Ramsay!

THE DYING SOLDIER TO HIS CHILD.

THESE eyes will soon be sightless,
  And soon this voice be dumb,
My darling, born beneath the flag,
  And cradled on the drum,
'Tis little I can leave thee
  Of wealth or worldly store,
But bear thou, with an honest name,
  The blade thy father bore.
I will not dwell on battles,
  Or sieges I have known,
I hope to join the Host of Saints
  Before the Great White Throne.
The cross is planted on thy brow,
  Oh! keep it undefiled:
The God of Battles, have in charge
  A dying soldier's child.
When flash the world's temptations,
  Unyielding pass them by,
And hold in all a soldier's scorn,
  The shadow of a lie.
A Christian and a soldier,
  Thou need'st not I should speak
Of comfort to the hapless due,
  And succour to the weak.

I cannot use a parson's words,
　Or like a parson pray;
The moral of a soldier's life
　I need not point to-day.
Be faithful to thy father's name,—
　Hark! hark! the evening gun,
Reveillé will not waken me,
　God guard a soldier's son.

THE OLD, OLD STORY.

YOUNG Willie was a cotter,
 He dwelt on Carron's Side,
He loved the winsome Maggie,
 And wooed her for his bride.

The maid was fair and fickle,
 And fain to flirt and jilt,
So Willie took the shilling
 And donned the plume and kilt.

Where lurks the branded tiger,
 Where roams the fierce Afghan,
For Willie grew the laurel wreath,
 In arid Hindostan.

There loomed strange tales of battle,
 Of holocausts of slain;
To many a Scottish home there came,
 Foreshadowing of pain.

Then Maggie hung her haughty head
 With sense of conscious guilt;
"Wae's me," she cried, "I slew with pride,
 The lad with plume and kilt."

They follow fast their pioneers,
   All evils that betide;
To many an ingle came there news—
   None came to Carron Side.

Deep sorrow preyed on Maggie's heart,
   And dimmed her sparkling eye,
"His blood," she said, "is on my head,
   My pride made Willie die.

"My happiness is gone for aye,
   Remorse must be my doom,
'Twas I laid low—no foreign foe—
   The lad with kilt and plume."

'Twas on a summer evening,
   The stars began to gleam,
A weary wanderer lagged behind
   The Carron's rapid stream.

She cried "Ah, me! I shattered
   The hopes on which he built,
His wraith will haunt me till I die,
   The lad with plume and kilt."

The wind was sadly soughing,
   The ripe moon's fitful beam
Threw oft a flickering shadow
   On Carron's rapid stream.

The maiden screamed with horror,
  Like tenant of the tomb,
There stood a kilted warrior,
  There waved a spectral plume.

" 'Tis his ! 'tis his ! " she murmured,
  And swooning with alarm,
She fell, the senseless maiden,
  Upon—a soldier's arm.

Oh ! precious were the accents,
  Like angels in a dream,
That woke to life the maiden
  By Carron's rapid stream.

" My bonnie, winsome, Maggie,
  In sunshine or in gloom,
Ye no forget the laddie
  That wears the kilt and plume ? "

Then smiling, weeping, sighing,
  She gave her plighted word,
One hand slipped from an epaulette,
  One rested on a sword.

Laudator Temporis acti.

WITH only one behind me,
    I've seen the column press,
In serried might, till shattered quite
    By Old Brown Bess;
Poor Brown Bess! somehow, I confess,
    I've a kind of sneaking weakness
For Old Brown Bess.

I've felt the breath of horses
    When swept in wild career,
(A brief eclipse of fiery lips)
    The charge of sword and spear;
Poor Brown Bess! at twenty feet or less,
    I've seen the saddles emptied
By Old Brown Bess.

Now war has lost its beauties,
    Gone is the well-dressed line,
O'er which when broke the battle's smoke
    Our level steel would shine;
Poor Brown Bess! they were like a board of chess,
    The natty squares that met the charge
With Old Brown Bess.

The front of war is altered:
  You scarcely see the foe
(Without a chance, with sword or lance)
  Your trigger-touch lays low.
Poor Brown Bess! what wonderful success
  I've known attend our Regiment
Arm'd with Old Brown Bess.

A BRISK AFFAIR AT THE FRONT.

TRANQUIL sinks the sun at even,
    Pace the sentries to and fro,
Group the picket close behind them
    Watching for the active foe.
Hark! a shot; no time for surmise,
    Grasp your rifles—start to foot:
"Ping," "ping," "ping," a rain of bullets!
    See the foe in full pursuit.
See the foe! But where detect him?
    Soldiers should be quick of touch,
Ever proof against surprises,
    Never prone to fire too much.
  *   *   *   *   *   *
  *   *   *   *   *   *
Mark the crafty, ambushed foeman,
    See the flash of restless eyes;
Steady aim at leisure taken
    And the baffled skulker dies.
Gather round the band triumphant,
    Drag the victim from his lair;
Mangling sore his lifeless body,
    They a horrid feast prepare.

Tell it not in prim dispatches,
   Should the foeman chance to fall,
Every gallant British soldier
   Straight becomes a Cannibal.
Wail my muse (so long exulting),
   In apologetic strain.
True it is; our valiant linesmen
   Feasted, glutted, o'er the slain.
Be the word of blame unspoken,
   Every soldier, small and big,
Vowed, his whistle slily whetting,
   Never was so nice—*a pig ! !*

THE ANCIENT REGIME.

HOWE'ER their epaulettes were gained,
   Who led us when we fought;
Though gold might their Commissions buy,
   Our hearts they never bought.
We loved the English gentlemen—
   Light heart and flashing eye—
Those gallant English gentlemen
   Who paid so much to die.
When danger lurked in fevered camp,
   Or revelled in the fray,
They never bade us go before,
   But ever led the way.
Whenever duty might be done,
   Or glory might be sought;
Though gold might their Commissions buy,
   Our hearts they never bought.
We loved those mettled dandies,
   Who never looked so well,
As when they smiled defiance on
   A shower of shot and shell.
Who might have led such lives at home,
   But served for next to naught;
Though gold might their Commissions buy,
   Our hearts they never bought.

THE CHAPLAIN'S SERMON.

JOSHUA V., ver. 13.

" Art thou for us, or for our adversaries ?"

THE Hymn's last note had died away;
The warriors scarred in many a fray,
At that blessed hour when labours cease,
Closed round the white-robed man of peace,
Who thus began, in accents low :—
"Say, for us art thou, or the foe?"

When Israel, once Egypt's slave,
In serried might crossed Jordan's wave,
A soldier, at a soldier's post,
The captain stalked about the host;
And thus he spake by Jericho,
"Say, for us art thou, or the foe?"

Well might he ask: before his eyes
A Warrior strode in martial guise;
All help, save God's was distant far,
And Israel was but young in war,
Well rang the Soldier's challenge so,
"Say, for us art thou, or the foe?"

(Ever in life when dangers lower,
When nerveless seems all human power;
When Satan's banners proudest fly,
Then legioned angels hover nigh)
" *Joshua, in me God's Captain know,*"
God for us! who need fear the foe?

Soldiers, still Joshua's war is ours,
With principalities and powers;
Jordan we cross for Canaan's shore,
Egypt behind, and doubt before;
Tossed by temptation to and fro,
For Jesus are we, or the foe?

Behold God's Captain at His post,
Closest at hand when needed most;
Challenge of faith He loveth well,
God with us is *Emanuel.*
Alone unaided? Soldier no!
God's Captain aids thee 'gainst the foe.

Kriege und Geschrei von Kriegen.

THE War-cry of España
　　May scare the Moorish horde;
The Battle-shout of gallant France
　　Has often been encored.

The deep *"Hoch! Hoch!"* of Germany,
　　The startled world has heard,
The *" Eljen,"* of Hungarian bands
　　The Magyar heart has stirred.

"Rockets" and *"Tigers"* may proclaim
　　Columbia's martial skill,
Italian *"Vivas"* learn to ring
　　From many a vine-clad hill.

But when from Britain's cohorts,
　　The loud *"Hurrahs!"* uprise,
Walhalla thunders with the sound,
　　And Vict'ry opes her eyes.

EVERY BULLET HAS ITS BILLET.

EVERY bullet has its billet,
  List the Soldier's simple creed;
Each must die when God shall will it,
  Who can shirk the fate decreed?

Be it on a bed of roses,
  Rampart-mound, or battle field;
'Tis our Father's will disposes,
  God decrees, and man must yield.

Why coquet with idle terror,
  Only once each mortal dies;
Never life knew greater error—
  Dread of possibilities.

Fear makes ill loom tenfold greater,
  Fear makes life a life-long death;
He who calls is the Creator;
  Careless draw a Soldier's breath.

Comes a sad foreboding? still it;
  There's no shirking cannon balls;
Every bullet has its billet
  Not by chance the Soldier falls.

MUSIC HATH CHARMS.

THEY say I've no notion of music,
　　Those exquisite dandies who play
On a weak concertina at sunset,
　　Or warble a Troubadour's lay.

My ear is attuned to the rattle
　　Of howitzer, rifle, and bomb ;
With the burst of the mine for the *forte*,
　　Piano, the roll of the drum.

I know not one note from the other !
　　To me, who the gamut learnt well,
From the treble "ping, ping," from the picket,
　　To the deep double-bass of the shell.

'Tis music the savage that charmeth
　　(Said Congreve)—no doubt he was right,
But the Congreve I knew dealt in rockets,
　　Their music astonished him quite.

I don't deny music is charming,
　If time, tune, and place serve aright,
But it roused me to positive ferment,
　The terrible music of fight.

But pardon the warmth of a soldier,
　The drum has entranced me too long;
When beauty the ramparts is manning,
　Who has not an ear for a song?

THE OLD TROOPER.

IT seems a dream of yesterday,
   The drum's harsh roar, the trumpet's bray,
    What time there met our view
The gallant Frenchman's dense array,
The squadrons marshalled for the fray,
    At placid Waterloo.

Where countless cannons' baleful breath
Left little seen save wounds and death,
    There passed in brief review,
I scarcely know of eye or ear,
A charge of horse in wild career,
    At reeking Waterloo.

I only know amidst the train
I dashed, I spurred,] I smote amain,
    And rode the squadrons through;
With echoing hoof and ringing cheer
We chased the Gallic cuirassier,
    At blood-stained Waterloo.

This frame is bowed by weight of years,
This body bears the print of spears,
    And sword cuts not a few;
This hand is palsied now by time,
It grasped an Eagle, in its prime,
    At glorious Waterloo.

TO AN ENQUIRING FOREIGNER.

WHAT colour are the British troops?
  A question hard to answer,
Because you see their colours wave
  From either Pole to Cancer;
Why! some are black, and some are white,
  And some are rather tawny,
And some are red, and some are grey,
  Besides Jack, Pat, and Sawney.

What stature are the British troops?
  To tell the truth they vary,
For some are giants in the land,
  And some are the contrary;
For some are slim, and some are fat,
  And some are fairly brawny;
All races serve within the ranks,
  Besides Jack, Pat, and Sawney.

What rations have the British troops?
  Whatever is in season,
Fish, flesh, and fowl (in divers lands)
  And fruit that grows the trees on;
And some drink water, some drink wine,
  And some drink brandy pawnee;
Besides the whiskey, and the beer
  That please Jack, Pat, and Sawney.

Bonus Pastor curat Oves.

OH! Father O'Flynn was the broth of a priest,
 Of spirit the highest, of stature the least,
On picking and stealing, and freedom of speech,
Oh! how he would lecture, and how he would
 preach.

His tongue it was sharp, but his smile it was
 bright;
His censure was heavy, his penance was light;
If ever in trouble his aid ye'd beseech,
How kindly he'd lecture, how gently would
 preach.

Your secrets he'd keep, and your letters indite,
But I rather suspect he'd a weakness for fight;
Should the dead and the dying lie thick in the
 breach,
Father Flynn would come running to shrive,
 not to preach.

Devoid of self-seeking—a stranger to fear,
He would fume under fire like a bold grenadier;
But the widow to comfort—the orphan to teach,
His life was a sermon—the best he could preach.

MALBROOK S'EN VA-T-À LA GUERRE.

NEVER sprang from author's whim
    Truer myth than honest Trim;
Slow of wit, to passion slow,
Corporal from top to toe.
Oft methinks I see him still,
Fashioned by primeval drill,
Humming some defiant lay
Of Ramilies or Malplaquet.
—Gaiters thirty buttons strong,
Pipeclayed belts, and pig-tail long;
Hat of most archaic cock,
Musket with its quaint flint lock.
Smiles provoke the costume quaint:
Who the inner man may paint?
Heart so large, so tender too,
Mind so simple, tongue so true.
Pity, on the watch to flow,
Love alike for friend and foe;
Patient, gentle, kindly Trim
At thy tears the eye grows dim;
Never Papal Bull were worse
Than thy wrath-extorted curse,
Malediction swift and strong
Wrung from guarded lips by wrong;
Ever Britain's soldiers be
Simple, modest, brave, like thee.

THE SOLDIER'S SWEETHEART.

THE harp she gently wooeth,
  The lassie I love well;
But most she loves the drum's fierce note,
  The haughty trumpet's swell.

In jewels though she blazeth
  And costly raiment wears;
She prizes most the tattered silk
  A young lieutenant bears.

A Dian swift she courseth,
  O'er hill and lea, and mead,
Yet loves she well the clash of steel
  And neighing of the steed.

Her face, where beauty reigneth,
  Smiles with a sweeter zest,
When set among the medals
  That deck a soldier's breast.

MATAGORDA.

AN INCIDENT OF THE PENINSULAR WAR.

NOT to the titled only
  Do noble hearts belong,
Full many a homely hero
  Evokes no tale, no song.

I sing a woman's action,
  A wife of low degree;
Judge if it be befitting,
  The page of chivalry.

We lay at Matagorda,
  Our force was seven score strong,
Of half a hundred cannon
  The roar was loud and long.

As lichen clings to ruins,
  We hugged the crumbling wall;
Nigh half our force disabled
  And pledged to slaughter all.

Full six times fell the banner,
　　The luckless flag of Spain,
Soon rooted to the very earth,
　　It braved the storm again.

With bluer blood than Spaniards',
　　Each inch of soil was wet,
And twice the sun had risen
　　And once the sun had set.

Yet ceased not for an instant
　　The discord of the fight;
The smoke obscured the noontide,
　　The shells illumed the night.

The tempest swept the rampart,
　　It shook the timeworn wall;
It failed to shake a woman's nerve,
　　Or woman's heart appal.

Sore need was there of water
　　When parched by wounds or strife;
Yet fifty cannon threatened
　　The golden bowl of life.

There looked a childlike drummer,
　　'Twas terrible to look;
So far the well—so fierce the storm,
　　The slender figure shook.

A woman took the bucket,
  Nor heeded shot and shell;
The wounded lay behind her,
  Before her lay the well.

She went—that dauntless woman,
  A smile her sole reward;
A shot the cable severed,
  But spared life's silver cord.

Again her burthen grasping,
  She paced that deadly track;
She drew the priceless water
  And came in safety back.

Oh! when ye read of David,
  Of water dear as life;
Record with Israel's heroes,
  Stout Ritson's gallant wife.

THE ARMY SERVICE CORPS.

THE soul of the Army's the four-wheeled
    Hussar,
The hands and the feet, and the stomach of war;
The heart of the linesman is gallant and high
When the crack of our whips tells that rations
    are nigh.
No trooper or guardsman, or blue-shirted tar,
Does more for the flag than the four-wheeled
    Hussar.

You may say what you will of support and relief
There's nothing supports you like grog, pork,
    and beef;
There is not a charger that owes us his whack,
But loves us much more than the brute on his
    back;
No marshal bejewelled with order and star,
So dear to the ranks as the four-wheeled Hussar.

While sqadrons press on, and their pathway
    is clear,
Have you never heard tell of a dash at the rear;
Then we get the worry, and they get the luck,
And the life of the Army depends on our pluck;
All the nice little strokes that may make, or
    may mar,
Hang just on the fate of the four-wheeled Hussar.

THE OLD WAR DOG.

BLACK Dawson had a secret,
   A secret none might know;
No laugh had he for jest or glee,
   No tear for tale of woe.

The wine-cup ne'er betrayed him,
   Nor woman's serpent wile;
His features, scarred by many a fray,
   Were strangers to a smile.

I saw him in the moment
   When glory came and praise:
Unheeded warrior's laurels
   Unheeded poet's bays.

I marked him in the moment,
   When down went many a file;
When every breath brought wounds and death—
   For once I saw him smile.

A SONG OF SERVICE.

THE 16TH LANCERS.

SING a song of Service—the Carbine and the
    Lance,
Of glory won 'neath India's sun, in Belgium,
    Spain, or France;
Let *Honour's Fountains* babble the feats of arms
    we wrought;
And *Victory's* own field record our terrible onslaught.

Sing a song of Service—what time with flowing
    rein,
And Lance in rest, we proudly swept that fatal
    Flemish plain;
Sing a song of Service, when on the Sutlej Banks,
We chased the Punjab chivalry, and broke the
    Khalsa ranks.

Sing a song of Service—the motto of our band,
"By sweep of spear in fleet career, or grapple
    hand to hand."
Behold our serried badges, by daring gained,
    not chance;
Sing a song of Service—the Carbine and the
    Lance.

QUATRE BRAS.

THE Squadron's mighty sweep—
  The Horseman's ringing cheer—
A sight that causes the heart to leap,
  A sound that gladdens the ear.

Again, and ever again,
  That terrible music swelled,
Till the nerves relaxed from the constant strain,
  And the war-worn ear rebelled;

Till the shoulder ached from the shot,
  And the weary eye sought rest;
No change in front from the battle's brunt
  And the flutter of plumèd crest.

Like a river bursting its banks,
  Like a whirling mass of snow;
On front and flanks of our feeble ranks,
  Resistless rushed the foe.

For God, and for Fatherland!
  For your proud historic name!
One more firm stand, heroic band!
  Stout heart and steady aim.

A pause—and a deadly peal,
  From front and flanks rings out;
A gasp, a gap, and a shiver of steel
  And a deafening English shout.

There warrior lay, and horse,
  Cuirass and pennon gay;
The Avalanche died to a snow-flake's force,
  And the billow wasted to spray.

Hurrah for the stedfast band,
  Whose doubled numbers show
A single heart for their Fatherland,
  A two-fold face to the foe.

MY REAR RANK MAN.

POOR Jack Day, in battle's deadly fray,
 How stoutly he would hold his own, how
sharply blaze away;
I never dreamt of danger, nor had a thought
 of fear,
The enemy before me, my comrade in the rear.
      Poor Jack Day.

Poor Jack Day, in India when I lay
A weary month in hospital, and seemed the
 earthworm's prey;
When dreams and facts were mingled, the first
 thing I espied,
Bowed down by manly sorrow, was my comrade
 by my side.
      Poor Jack Day.

Poor Jack Day, when we dragged our weary way,
Through forests where the mighty trees obscured
 the light of day;
With ready wit and willing aid, the march he
 would beguile,
And his song would lure the laggard for many
 a toilsome mile.
      Poor Jack Day.

Poor Jack Day, when becalmed in Table Bay,
His " heavy shotted hammock " roused the tears
   of Ocean's spray;
The reg'ment ceased its laughter, and the
   seaman's oath was stayed,
I'd rather be his front-rank man than Gen'ral
   of Brigade.

                       Poor Jack Day.

THE ROYAL MARINE.

THAT thorough Sea Lion, the plucky Amphion
    'S the type of a Royal Marine, sir;
When taken on board, he with music was stored,
    Quite a dabster at " God save the Queen," sir.

When the crew let him shift, aye! and cut
    him adrift,
    Why, he charmed all the fish in the ocean;
And a dolphin, they say, took him up on his way,
    With a singular sort of devotion.

When the Royal Marine on the Ocean is seen
    No man in the service is smarter,
Should our venturesome foes come to traffic
    in blows;
    They will find they've to deal with a Tartar.

On sea, mud, or land, where to float, wade,
    or stand,
    He's as handy as ancient Amphion;
Ship, camp, or redoubt, you can ne'er throw
    him out,
    Of Odin this thorough-bred scion.

On land, mud, or sea, with song, jest, and glee,
    Amphion-like he will be seen, sir;
He's never at fault, parade, or assault,
    Your well set-up Royal Marine, sir.

A VETERAN'S TALE.

OH! would ye hear of those we met,
With musket, sabre, bayonet?
List to a soldier's simple strain:
The foe was France, the scene was Spain.

'Twixt hostile camp and British hold
A broad and rapid river rolled;
Secure, our force the foe defied,
But they were French on yonder side.

All honour to the sixty brave,
Who naked, dared the rapid wave;
Tooth clutching steel, their packs before
They push, and swimming gain the shore.

No thought to dress, no time to form;
The tower the dripping warriors storm.
His tribute let a Briton pay
To Gallic pluck and brave Guingret.

ELEGY.

WHERE do they sleep, the comrades tried,
In youth, who pressed on either side;
In duty's cause who fought and bled,
And never flinched when honour led?

Go, ask the arid hills of Spain
How many fell—nor fell in vain,
What time our march from Lisbon's wall,
By many windings led to Gaul.

Ask Afric, or the Morning land,
Or where Acadian forests stand;
Where Indus rolls his rapid wave,
Too frequent mark the soldier's grave.

The sun (of life to come that speaks)
On ocean plains or mountain peaks
Scarce rises, but his rays illume
Some gallant comrade's nameless tomb.

But why should idle tears be shed?
Who live in fame are scarcely dead;
While trumpet sounds or colour flies,
A British regiment never dies.

WOMAN.

THE kettledrums are sounding,
Our gallant steeds are bounding;
And girls and boys, with cheery noise,
The squadron are surrounding.

How is it at the parting;
Unbidden tears are starting?
'Tis woman's eyes that mock the skies,
Her rainbow glances darting.

In triumph home returning,
What rivals India's burning
On cheek and brow? the thought that now
For each some fair is yearning.

If 'midst the dead and dying,
The wounded brave be lying;
Come life, come death, 'tis woman's breath
That comfort is supplying.

Sergeant-Major SMITH on COMPETITIVE EXAMINATION.

I'M nothing but a grey moustache,
  And sentiment is strange to me;
Of scholar's lore small is my store
Of figures or geography.
  Figures and geography! figures and geography!
I've got by heart what I impart
  Of figures and geography.

I've served in India, China too,
New Zealand, and Ameriky;
There is no map my skill can cap
In figures and geography.
  Figures and geography! figures and geography!
I've got by heart what I impart
  Of figures and geography.

A ball I from the Russians had,
A Sowar's blade disabled me,
A Nigger's knife assailed my life,
While studying geography.
  Figures and geography! figures and geography!
My wounds will tell I've studied well
  Figures and geography.

A LEGEND OF DARTMOOR.

7TH. FUSILEERS.

'TIS not alone when banners wave,
And shouts of battle rouse the brave,
When triumph's accents rend the sky,
The soldier nobly learns to die.

If laurels deck the hero's plume,
Not wreathless be the martyr's tomb ;
Yet strangers oft to fame or thanks
They fall—the martyrs of the ranks.

The sun was low, the scene was wild,
The driven snow in mounds was piled;
With sable clouds was Dartmoor crowned,
An Arctic desert lay around.

Warm housed at home, the peasant hears
Their muffled tread—three Fusileers ;
The bear-skin, like an alp of snow,
Towered o'er a wintry realm below.

And as they breathed, fantastic gloom
Wound round them, like the wraith of doom.
"Stay," said the kindly peasant, "Stay,
A world of snow obstructs the way.

"No beacon light your steps to guide,
The night so wild, the plain so wide;
Shake from each helm its snowy crest,
And share to-night a cotter's rest."

They answered, not with sighs or tears,
Those simple stedfast Fusileers—
"Nor night, nor death can soldiers stay,
We have our orders, and obey."

When broke the half reluctant day,
The shepherd on his anxious way,
Marked three small cairns of driven snow,
And three stout soldiers slept below.

The fame of one devoted soul,
Depends not on a Battle Roll;
In death they speak to after years,
Those simple, stedfast Fusileers.

I know not if one sculptured stone
Records the fact, to angels known;
Their crown of glory ne'er shall fade,
Who had their orders, and obeyed.

CHANT DE DEPART.

FAREWELL, England, lost to view at sea,
  Absence closer binds us, hallowed land, to
thee;
Farewell England, wheresoe'er we roam,
True as needle to the pole, the soldier turns
  to home.
                    Farewell, England, &c.

Farewell, England, volunteers are we,
Freely in thy service we cross the foaming sea;
True, we take our country everywhere we go,
English hearts go after us, happen weal or woe.
                    Farewell, England, &c.

Farewell, England, proudly may we boast,
Distant is the warfare that guards thy sacred coast;
Proud thy Island charter—where thy banners wave,
Shrinks the fell dominion of tyrant over slave.
                    Farewell, England, &c.

Farewell, England, may we soon again,
Crowned with wreaths of laurel, cross the stormy
main ;
Flash the hostile sabre, hiss the hostile ball,
We'll come back victorious, or come not back
at all.

> Farewell, England, &c.

Farewell, England, speedy come the day,
When press exulting bands of friends to break
our firm array ;
That firm array of volunteers, who fight for duty's
sake,
No burst of shell or dash of shot, or sabre
stroke could break.

> Farewell, England, &c.

INKERMAN.

ONE dark November morning,
    The Russ burst on our sight;
Our files were few and feeble
    And fierce the Muscovite;
The place we took at sun-rise,
    That place we held at night.

Worn down were we by watching,
    Scant fare and clothing light;
A mass of foes assailed our front
    And menaced left and right;
The place we took at sun-rise,
    That place we held at night.

Then roared the cannons' thunder,
    Then gleamed the sabre bright;
As fed by numberless reserves
    Pressed on the Russian fight;
The place we took at sun-rise,
    That place we held at night.

Our cartridges exhausted,
 Wherewith to fell or smite,
We grasped, and stock and steel repelled
 The stubborn Muscovite;
The place we took at sun-rise,
 That place we held at night.

Oh! timely was the succour,
 And matchless the delight,
When rent and torn the foe recoiled,
 Ourselves exhausted quite;
The place we took at sun-rise,
 That place we held at night.

IMPOSSIBLE.

IMPOSSIBLE! you raw recruit,
  Where *did* you get that word?
I've heard strange oaths in twice ten years,
  That phrase I never heard.

Impossible! why reckon guns,
  Or count brigades of men?
What odds if they are ten to one,
  Why! aren't you one to ten?

Take comfort lad—with bayonet fixed,
  When rushing on the foe;
For every step you take in line,
  You've just one less to go.

And think of this at anytime,
  If fears oppress your mind;
Ten foes in front aren't half as bad
  As only one behind.

Impossible! with thrust of steel,
  Or shoulder pressed to gun;
A stedfast eye, a steady hand,
  And nothing can't be done.

Impossible! with words like that,
  No feats of arms were wrought;
Don't waste your time in counting heads,
  You spoke before you thought.

THE RIGHT SORT.

YOU ask me for adventures—for tales of blood
    and storm,
Of what has chanced in twice ten years I've
    worn my uniform;
I've seen, God knows, a many things, from rise
    to set of sun,
The regiment did its duty well, I don't know
    much I've done.

I've tracked the wily Maori in his tangled forest
    home,
I've marked from Cape Coast Castle, the Southern
    Ocean's foam;
I've chased the tawny traitor on India's burning
    strand,
And I have stood on Alma's ridge when few
    were spared to stand.

I've done as much in Persia as others dared to do,
And proud Magdala's crested height has burst
    upon my view;
My tramp has roused the languid air, in distant,
    quaint Hong-Kong,
The solemn pines of Acadie have echoed back
    my song.

I might have seen some wondrous things if mine
    were better sight,
Whate'er men say who stop at home you don't
    see much in fight;
I've heard the slogan of the charge—seen foes in
    full retreat,
Short commons I have often known—I never
    knew defeat.

THE SCOTS GREY.

ASK why do I cease from my labour so soon ;
Have you never heard tell of the Eighteenth
of June?
Ah! England may fairly be proud of that day,
And the terrible! terrible! horses of grey.

Whatever our exploits, the world, do you see,
Thought the troopers of France were far better
than we ;
But what said their chief when he saw our array?
"Those terrible! terrible! horses of grey."

An onslaught more dashing there never was
made,
Than the furious charge of the Union Brigade;
But the eye might discern in the heart of the fray
Those terrible! terrible! horses of grey.

Then the sabre was queen over carbine and spear,
And the roar of the cannon was drowned in
our cheer ;
Then the wave of confusion was flecked like the
spray
By those terrible! terrible! horses of grey.

And Buonaparte watched our triumphant career,
When the champions of France turned post-haste
　　to the rear;
And it was not good-nature that forced him
　　to say,
" Those terrible! terrible! horses of grey!"

ADIEU.

THE trumpets are braying,
  Our chargers are neighing;
Too long I am staying,
  So potent the spell.
The lips' tender pressing,
The hands' last caressing—
And then, my fond blessing,
  My darling, farewell!

Be the heart high, love,
Stifle the sigh, love;
Tearless the eye, love,
  Aye shall it be.
Come life or death, love,
To my last breath, love,
Steadfast my faith, love,
  Worthy of thee.

CORUÑA.

BRISK the foemen were pursuing,
   Springless steps and accents low,
Spoke how much our hearts were rueing,
   Face to coast and back to foe.

Trumpets sound advance to glory,
   Hearts are high and motions fleet;
Ah! how altered is the story
   Of an army in retreat.

Baffled by o'erpowering numbers,
   Hampered by a cold ally;
Crushed by all the mind that cumbers,
   Back we turned to do or die.

Curses on a friend half-hearted,
   Curses on perfidious Spain!
Full of confidence we started,
   Hopeless turned we back again.

Spake our leader, sorely slandered,
   Braver bosom never beat—
" Sacred be each gun and standard,
   Doubly sacred in retreat."

"On," he cried, "behind, around us,
  Lower the mountains, press the foes,
Common ill hath closely bound us,
  Common pluck shall earn repose."

So we gained by firm endurance,
  Dauntless bearing to the foe,
Mountain crest, in full assurance
  Britain's fleet to hail below.

Wind and water, servants willing
  Of some favoured child of war
(Measure of our woe upfilling),
  Kept our ships detained afar.

Never Poet's wildest dreaming,
  Song of Scald or Troubadour,
Had a Hero more beseeming
  Than our leader, fearless Moore.

Failed to meet his eager glancing
  Britain's flag 'twixt main and sky;
Turned he on the foe advancing,
  Resolute to do or die.

Oh! that bitter hour of trial,
  Ruin come, with succour nigh;
Luring first, then stern denial,
  Leagued against him earth and sky.

Made at ease our line's formation,
  Came no onslaught unforescen;
Shade of doubt or hesitation
  Never dulled our hero's mien.

Calm he saw the bold pursuer
  Burst in vain on British steel;
Saw that brave unflinching Moore,
  Squadrons halt and standards reel.

Slowly sank our stricken leader,
  Saved his army, saved his fame;
Ne'er in hist'rys page the reader
  Lights upon a nobler name.

Towering over base detraction,
  Sans réproche, like him of yore;
Worse than mortal wound in action,
  Were the inward chafes before.

Patient victor—rest in glory,
  England still thy name reveres;
Poet's lay, and soldier's story,
  Rouse our sympathetic tears.

PEACE AND WAR.

THE life of the Soldier 's the model of life,
  For whose is the lot without trouble and
  strife ?
In all our engagements the world follows suit,
And every child born is another recruit.

The life of the Soldier 's the model of life;
If we have our foes, every cit has a wife ;
E'en the richest of men—give the Devil his due,
Finds the longest of lives is one constant review.

The lot of the Soldier 's a model for all,
For what is the day but some rise and some fall;
In the Church, in the State, in the Mart, in
  the Street,
Some vanquish, some fail, some advance, some
  retreat.

The Parson will tell you that life's a campaign,
The Merchant's at war for his credit and gain;
The Lawyer, God help him, fights hard for his fee,
And his tongue has more awe than a cannon
  for me.

The life of the Soldier 's the model of life,
Every two of each trade wage a war to the knife;
But the heart of the Soldier more chivalry knows,
For when we cease firing, we cease to be foes.

MY LITTLE BLACK MARE.

MY little black mare—my bonny black
mare,
Dick Turpin's was never a better, I swear;
One touch of the rein, and one hint of the spur,
And trench, sword, or bayonet, never stopped her.
To ride down the squadron, to sweep through
the square,
Oh! give me the bound of my bonny black mare.

She'd a grace most bewitching, a heart that
could feel,
And her ear was entranced by the clashing of
steel.
No lute had such charms to the ear of the fair,
As the note of the charge to my bonny black
mare.

When my arm was uplifted to ward or to smite,
She would swerve, she would snort, she would
rear, she would bite;
My comrades would cheer, and the foemen would
stare,
At the pluck and the dash of my bonny black
mare.

When we closed with the foe, what a bad one
    to beat,
What a laggard was she at the sound of retreat;
But, thanks be to God, such a summons was rare
To the trooper in blue, and his bonny black mare.

We've shared the same fortune, through thick
    and through thin,
For a speck on her coat there's a seam in my
    skin ;
Come weal or come woe, my all I would share,
With my fourfooted comrade, my bonny black
    mare.

A BOSOM FRIEND.

I DON'T admire your cynic,
　　With his sneer and ugly frown;
Who never cries a neighbour up,
　　But always runs him down.

I've just one staunch companion,
　　Of honest, kindly mien;
O'er land and sea he sticks to me,
　　My little, black Dudeen.

'Tis true, I treat him roughly,
　　A weed his only fare;
But while he hangs upon my lips,
　　He has no other care.

And when his task is ended,
　　He dwells beside my heart;
Come weal, come woe, I love him so,
　　We two can never part.

In peace he's not the smartest,
　　But under fire he's clean;
We all are clay the parsons say,
　　And so's my black Dudeen.

Should rations ever fail us,
　　Or pork and beef be tough,
To stay a soldier's stomach,
　　He cannot do enough.

Oh! what a constant friend he is,
　　How true he aye hath been;
Come day, come night, his smile is bright,
　　My little black Dudeen.

In days of active service,
　　In piping times of peace,
He soothes a soldier's sorrows,
　　And bids his joys increase.

A prey to disappointment,
　　Or victim to the spleen,
My spirits rise when vapour flies
　　From out my dear Dudeen.

I do not care for pipe-clay,
　　It lost me once a stripe;
But dearer than my rifle
　　I hold my good clay-pipe.

He is steadfast, he is loyal,
　　And devoted to the Queen;
He burns to pay a tax each day,
　　My little black Dudeen.

NULLI SECUNDUS.

IT may be true we're number two;
  With bayonet or gun, sir,
I'd have you know, both friend and foe,
  We're second just to none, sir.

Whate'er the time, in Arctic clime,
  Or 'neath an Eastern sun, sir,
Both black and white have felt our might;
  We're second just to none, sir.

Our battle flag—that glorious rag,
  We'll follow it like fun, sir;
In field or trench, 'gainst Russ or French,
  We're second just to none, sir.

Whene'er drums beat, there's no retreat,
  Until our work be done, sir;
In battle fray, be first who may,
  We're second just to none, sir.

THE SOLDIER'S DREAM.

THE watch-fire was flamin' when I took to
    dhramin',
I might have been dhrinkin', I ralely can't tell;
When glory's a bamin', it's asy work dhramin',
    If you dont git a fact, let a dhrame do as well;
If y're sick or y're sore, think of plinty, galore!
    Jist hear what, in fancy, a souldier befell.

I dhramed of a place like the Palace at Sydenham,
    Where monsters move slower than we can
        stand still;
The quarest I saw (don't I wish w'd got rid
        on him)
    Was that wonderful bullock for souldiers they
        kill.
On his hide was a mark that he got in the ark,
    And he sucked up the salt wid the deuce
        of a will.

In a hogshead of brine there were swimmin'
        some swine;
    That divils got in 'em was likely enough,
(Small power to their taste, for the divil a baste
    But a souldier could do wid a morsel so tough);
And a Jew or a Turk might have aten that pork,
    And never smelt pig in the wonderful stuff.

There were cats of noin tales, both ladies and
    males,
    And crinkums and crankums I'd like well
      to loot;
And there was Brown Bess in the natest of veils,
    And a son of a gun was preferrin' his suit;
I knew she could rattle, when dhrums beat
    to battle,
    But she romped in could blood like a Cockney
    recruit.

I was narely mistakin' the dhramin' for wakin',
    The things that I saw were so mighty jintale;
And I've got a notion, by way of promotion,
    I'd have blossomed in epeaulettes, goulden
    and rale;
But them salty creations, they sarve out for
    rations
    Made me wake up quite dhry wid a cravin'
    for ale.

ICH DIEN.

LITTLE need of fabled story,
 List the tale our banners tell;
They have waved o'er carnage gory,
 Comrades old of shot and shell.

Oft have Cambria's Minstrels, hoary,
 Hymn'd the warrior's deathless name;
See our records mute of glory,
 Silent heralds of our fame.

Mark our Prince's ancient token,
 Nobly won in tented field;
Honour's chain is still unbroken,
 Never knight had richer shield.

Minden yields her wreath of roses,
 Laurels spring from hilly Spain;
Every war a badge imposes,
 Honour is not woo'd in vain.

When the British guns are roaring,
 Near or distant be the scene,
Mark our standards proudly soaring,
 Read our haughty boast, "*Ich dien.*"

CONNAUGHT "ROBBERS."

OH! the brave Eighty-eighth are the dread
    of the foe,
And, in turn, they fear naught save the deuce
    and provo'
For you see all our time's so devoted to fightin',
That *meum* and *tuum* we take no delight in.

Now, what you call time was not made for
    a Ranger,
Our clock only strikes at the moment of danger;
At the face of a foe, or an enemy's larder,
Only give us the word, and we cannot strike
    harder.

We heroes in line are so bold in attacks, sir,
All the clothes on the line get to stick to our
    backs, sir;
Whatever is fittest for eating and drinking,
Just jumps in our way, quick as speaking or
    thinking.

There is not a thing that is sold or is bought,
But is proud to belong to a lad of Connaught;
Mere picking up turkeys and geese is not looting,
But a tribute we pay to the bravelike saluting.

We are rascals and thieves, rather brigands
    than not,
Since the enemy's rations fall into our pot;
When the path of the flag with destruction is
    fraught,
Then " Faugh-a-ballagh " for the lads of
    Connaught.

MARCHING CHORUS.

BEAT the drums before us,
Wave our banners o'er us;
    Front and rear
    Return the cheer,
Then raise the soldiers' chorus.
        Beat the drums before us, &c.

The mothers free that bore us
As freemen still may score us;
    A volunteer
    Knows naught of fear,
So raise the soldiers' chorus.
        Beat the drums before us, &c.

The woods and rocks sonorous,
Shall echo back the chorus;
    Our ears have known
    A harsher tone,
So raise the soldiers' chorus.
        Beat the drums before us, &c.

Ave Victoria Imperator—Morituri te Salutant.

WHEN, decked in our smartest,
   We pass in review,
To show the beholder
   What Britons can do ;
Our belts at their whitest,
   Our blades bright and keen,
We shout with devotion,
    " Hurrah! for the Queen."

When men black with powder,
   And steeds white with foam,
Sweep on to destruction,
   For duty and home ;
Ever true to one purpose,
   Though altered the scene,
We shout with devotion,
    " Hurrah ! for the Queen."

www.ingramcontent.com/pod-product-compliance
Lightning Source LLC
Chambersburg PA
CBHW032151010726
47493CB00008BA/2660